# Found
# Lives

# FOUND
❧ ❦ ❧
# LIVES

*A Collection of Found Photographs*

JAMES NOCITO

First Edition

0I 00 99 98  4 3 2 I

This is a Peregrine Smith Book, published by
Gibbs Smith, Publisher
P.O. Box 667
Layton, UT 8404I

Edited by Gail Yngve
Designed by James Nocito
and Persimmon Graphics

Some quotes in this work appeared originally in other works: the Renee Vivien quote is from *The Muse of the Violets*, translated by Margaret Porter and Catherine Kroger; Naiad Press, 1977; used here with the permission of the publisher. The Duane Michals quote is used with the permission of the author.

Printed in Hong Kong

Library of Congress Cataloging-in-Publication Data

Nocito, James, 1960—
Found Lives / James Nocito. — 1st ed.
p.   cm.
"A Peregrine Smith book"—T.p. verso.
ISBN 0–87905–6I8–5
I. Photographs—Catalogs. 2. Photographs—Collectors and collecting. I. Title
TRI99.N63 1998
779'.074—dc2I                    97–38695
                    CIP

Acknowledgments

For their generous support and advice, my sincere thanks to Susan Brandabur, Midge and Mark Caparosa, Hillary Carlip, Peggy Conklin, Julia Doughty, Richard Fischer, Andrea Hattersley, Hayley Mitchell, Lance Moles, the Nocito Family, Gary Piepenbrink, Diane Scott, Sue Sillano, Judith Sieck, Liz Szabla, Jonathan Westover, and Gail Yngve.

I am especially grateful to Eileen Boniecka for her enormous efforts and assistance.

This book is dedicated to Sal Montagna.

# CONTENTS

Introduction — vii

Talking Pictures — 1

Family Album — 19

Found Lives — 37

Women — 55

Men — 67

Children — 79

Love — 93

*We must pay attention so as not to be deceived by the familiar.*
—Duane Michals

These pictures are worthless. Stuffed into shoe boxes and relegated to the lowliest position at swap meets and junk stores, they are disregarded, overlooked, and rarely even priced. When a few are rescued from oblivion and presented for purchase, an interesting improvisation often follows. Their value has never been considered. After a deal has been struck, the question arises from the seller: "What do you do with those things?"

An eccentric friend gave me my first found photo when I was in high school. She read Camus and wore her grandmother's sweaters, but even so I found it truly strange that she would fixate on this picture of a person she never knew, someone presumably dead. It was a picture of a foreign-looking soldier, stern and proud beyond his years and height, comical and frightening at once. This was an object whose value had expired, as meaningless as a stranger's memories. Yet there was a humanity about it, and its very anonymity made it universal. I was hooked.

After years of collecting, the question remained: "What do I do with them?" I've photocopied elements and incorporated them into collages, enlarged and displayed them, and in rare unproprietary moments, given some away. I've done drawings and woodcuts of a few, but they resist my efforts to interpret them in other media. More than anything, I love getting lost in them, or watching someone else become absorbed, touched, or amused.

The photos I've selected here were chosen for a variety of reasons. Some work purely on an abstract level. In some cases this may certainly be attributed to accident. Others are clearly posed, but full of mysterious information. What were these people doing? What were their relationships to one another? Who was behind the camera, and what was he or she seeing at that moment? These pictures reveal their secrets slowly or not at all. But when poring over them, I am always astounded by the perfection of their composition: the arc of trees that ends at a central figure's head, the shadows and shapes that dominate the frame. Studying them is not unlike staring at the flawless imperfections of a leaf. Their existence seems predetermined, and since the photographers are unknown, they have their own independent life, unattached to a human creator. And yet, they are as common and expendable as a leaf.

What can we learn from these pictures? What can they teach us, these stray bits of our history? They belong to all of us, these images of nameless, ordinary people who worked and ate and hoped and laughed; they carved out an existence and occasionally found time to enjoy themselves. They loved their children. They had dignity. They died.

These pictures are of us. Enjoy them.

# TALKING PICTURES

Louella wrote a simple novel
called *Willow Be My Garland*
and no one in Saginaw paid it much mind
except to say they were glad
somebody in that family was good for something
'cause it surely wasn't farming.

Quite without her permission
the novel was adapted to a play.
She discovered this
when a troupe of actors from Ann Arbor
appeared at her door.

They took her to Lake Huron
calling her "Dame Louella"
and at the water's edge
acted out her play,
which now contained a lengthy love scene.

On the long ride home
Louella devised the plots
for her next four novels
and the rest of her life.

I bet Louisa a dime to do it.
She said, "You best be prepared
to marry me, too. Nobody
disturbs Mama's reading.
She'll run me out of the house."
But her mama hardly budged.
"Child, you know I've got eyes back there,"
she said
and kept on reading.

After, Louisa said, "Keep your dime.
I haven't seen her smile like that
since the porch swing fell under Jeffrey."

I think I will marry Louisa.
Anyone who can see a smile
on that woman
has an extra set of eyes herself,
eyes that I want
looking at me.

The house looks different now.
Sold the piano
and boarded up the closets
'cause they charge less tax that way.
And I took on a boarder
who hangs magazine pictures on the wall.
You wouldn't recognize the bedroom.
But I keep your chair
by the window.
I tell people it will break
if they try to sit in it.
Once I opened the window
and sat nearby
and maybe it was the wind
that caused the chair to stir.
Somebody might have been burning leaves outside.
That might explain the curl of smoke
floating in the air
just as though it came
from your cherry-wood pipe.
But I said, "Hello, John Samuel.
Ain't the breeze lovely?"

It was all her idea
to sew pilgrim outfits
and make Uncle August wear a headdress.
Then came time to kill the turkey
and something snapped in her.
She stomped and wailed
about God's small creatures
and how she was going to set that bird free.
"Go on, girl," they all said, "stop that fool!"
I just watched from the back porch,
pretending not to understand.

I was so scared he'd think I was too plain
that I cried
the whole train ride.
But I guess he thought I looked all right.
We got married the next day.

Still, he didn't say more than
a few dozen words
the first month I lived here.
He don't use up kindling
when building a house,
just like he said in the newspaper ad.
And he wasn't lying
about living simple, either.

Then out of the blue one day
he says we're going for a ride
to Archangelo's Bridge.
Nobody built it.
It's just that way.

Since that day
I don't miss home so bad.
You should see his face, Mama.
It's a good face.
And his smile is something to see.
Since that day on Archangelo's Bridge
I don't miss home, just you.

She wasn't joking
when she said
anyone could tell you where her tent was.

Nothing in Calvin's experience
prepared him for a weekend
at an artists' colony
with Rosabelle and George.

The question is
"Where is George?"
He was in the
boat when I took
the picture.
Come and see
us at Chautauqua.
Anyone can
tell you where
our tent is.
R. B.

A year after she was widowed
at the age of forty-three,
she met a riverboat gambler
who didn't care about the odds.

When he invited her aboard his boat
she asked, "What kind of name
is 'The Elder'?
If it were to me
I'd call it 'Second Wind.'"

They were married before spring ended.

On "The Elder"

Everyone was in such a funny mood
on Grandma's birthday.
Three times I asked Mama,
"How old is Grandma?"
and she shushed me every time.

Hardly nobody was talking
except Uncle Harmon.
"Gummin' on, as usual," Mama'd say.
This time it was small-game hunting.
He kept saying,
"After many a-summer dies the swan,"
which was making Grandma awful cross.
I could tell.

Then when Grandma put the pheasant on the table,
Uncle Harmon said the swan thing again
and it was one too many times for Grandma.

She said, "By heaven, Harmon,
if you say that one more time,
I'll brain you."

I didn't think much could shock my Mama,
but it took her days to recover.

FAMILY ALBUM

Look at them. Smiling like they're the most normal family in the world. I know better because I watch them and I listen, too. From the top of the stairway, in darkened halls, I hear all the secrets I'm too young to understand.

Aunt Mamie, for instance, always takes on the appearance of the flowers in her yard. She looked positively demented the year she grew hydrangeas. But the following summer, she grew agapanthas. It nearly killed her.

Aunt Mamie blanched when she saw Uncle Wendell sneaking off to a meeting for the Secret Fellowship of the Brothers of Agamemnon—membership: three.

"What in creation?" she cried, her voice trembling with jealousy that her own husband, a bank teller who read scripture to the congregation on Sundays, was secretly even battier than she.

Morticians are always a little weird, but the ocean air did crazy things to Uncle Archibald. He made us stand around him and pray as the tide moved slowly in. . . .

After the war, Great Uncle Eugene lost no battles. Cousin Gerald once called him the Little Colonel, then walked with a limp to an early grave.

Sure enough, ten years later cousin Edna found
a man who did the same.

Everyone said poor Aunt Constance was made of patience, married to a man like Roscoe. The ladies in her Bible group prayed that there'd be a moment's rest for her someday. Truth is, in private, she liked to tease up her hair, gulp saki, and tell jokes that scared the holy hell out of Roscoe. He never let on, even when he outlived her. "My woman was a saint," he said at the wake, gently placing a red tortoise-shell comb into her casket.

He spent his days squinting at life in the far distance. Then, the summer of his thirty-seventh year in the lighthouse, Uncle Webster put down his binoculars, left his post, put on Sunday clothes, told his mother he needed to buy kerosene, and walked down to the docks. A French yacht had dropped anchor there, and when the party aboard saw Webster, they thought he was a local dignitary bidding them welcome. He was given the seat of honor next to the proud host, Monsieur de Germain.

Just mentioning his name makes people feel awkward. No word in seven years, not so much as a postcard.

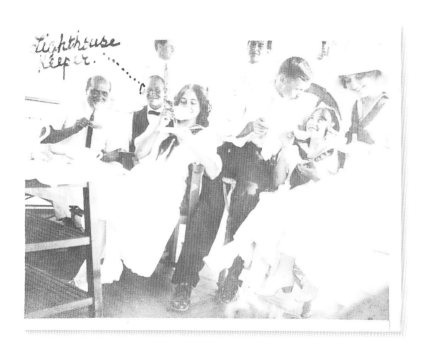

Lighthouse
Keeper.

FOUND LIVES

Johnny & a couple of Friends playing
Cow boys on a farm In California

R232

Anna
Edith Ward
Margaret
drying hair

900 north
Edward St
Decatur

Bob —

Sun bath
on my bed.

This is about how I
looked when you seen me
last aint it Frank?

This is the Picture we took at the ranch of myself and the three Boys. How are they is Claire still waiting for Cal to Come Back

A 40

"Fish is gold" –
here.

On my trip to europe
I don't know which
way we were going
When this was taken

My guest for seven weeks who returned to her home in Havana, Cuba, for Thanksgiving. She is a rare delight—

1930—

# WOMEN

Best friend, my well-spring in the wilderness.

George Eliot
*The Spanish Gypsy*

Serene I fold my hands and wait,
Nor care for wind nor tide nor sea;
I rave no more 'gainst time or fate,
For lo! my own shall come to me.

John Burroughs
"Waiting"

A man is as good as he has to be, and a woman as bad as she dares.

Elbert Hubbard
*Epigrams*

A good rest is half the work.

Yugoslav Proverb

What is it that pulls me away from what others call happiness, home and loved ones, why does my love for them not hold me down, root me? Games. Adventures. The unknown.

Anaïs Nin
*The Diaries of Anais Nin, Vol. II*

# Men

Men, my brothers, men the workers, ever reaping something new
Than which they have done but earnest of the things that they shall do:
For I dipt into the future, far as human eye could see,
Saw the Vision of the world, and all the wonder that would be.

Alfred Lord Tennyson
"Locksley Hall"

Man is a rope connecting animal and superman—a rope over a precipice. . . . What is great in man is that he is a bridge and not a goal.

Friedrich Nietzsche
*Thus Spake Zarathustra*

True friendship is of royal lineage. It is of the same kith and breeding as loyalty and self-forgetting devotion and proceeds upon a higher principle even than they. For loyalty may be blind, and friendship must not be; devotion may sacrifice principles of right choice which friendship must guard with an excellent and watchful care.

Woodrow Wilson
*Baccalaureate Sermon,*
*Princeton University, May 9, 1907*

A broad margin of leisure is as beautiful in a man's life as in a book.

Henry David Thoreau
*Journal*

If a body's ever took charity, it makes a burn that don't come out.

John Steinbeck
*The Grapes of Wrath*

# CHILDREN

A Child of Happiness always seems like an old soul living in a new body, and her face is very serious until she smiles, then the sun lights up the world.

Anne Cameron
*Daughters of Copper Woman*

A child's attitude toward everything is an artist's attitude.

Willa Cather
*The Song of the Lark*

The natural impulse of my being, from my earliest recollection, was—not to observe others—but to flow into them.

Romain Rolland
*Journey Within*

We should not make light of the troubles of children. They are worse than ours, because we can see the end of our troubles and they can never see any end.

William Middleton
quoted in *Autobiography* by W. B. Yeats

The child, if it were a philosopher, might say to us: "You laugh at me because I am so absorbed in make-believe, but you do not laugh at yourselves, though you are equally absorbed in make-believe.  You, no more than I, have found the key to what is permanent, but live seriously in a world of playthings."

Robert Lynd
*The Peal of Bells*

There was a time when meadow, grove, and stream,
The earth, and every common sight,
To me did seem
Apparelled in celestial light
The glory and the freshness of a dream.

William Wordsworth
"Ode: Intimations of Immortality
from Recollections of Early Childhood"

# LOVE

But Cupid is a downy cove,
Wot it takes a lot to hinder,
And if you shuts him out o' the door,
Vy he valks in at the vinder.

J. R. Planché
"The Discreet Princess"

To be in love is merely to be in a state of perceptual anesthesia—to mistake an ordinary young man for a Greek god or an ordinary young woman for a goddess.

H. L. Mencken
*Prejudices*

If two stand shoulder to shoulder against the gods,
Happy together, the gods themselves are helpless
Against them, while they stand so.

Maxwell Anderson
*Elizabeth the Queen*

Our love is part of infinity,
Absolute as death and beauty. . .
See, our hearts are joined and our hands are united
Firmly in space and in eternity.

> Renee Vivien,
> "Union" in *The Muse of the Violets*
> translated by Margaret Porter
> and Catherine Kroger

As one who cons at evening o'er an album all alone,
And muses on the faces of the friends that he has known,
So I turn the leaves of Fancy till, in shadowy design,
I find the smiling features of an old sweetheart of mine.

James Whitcomb Riley
"An Old Sweetheart of Mine"